Faro Sent His Horse
Slowly Ahead,

silently urging it to be damned careful about where it put its feet. His right boot swung over the edge of the trail, the left from time to time scraped the near-vertical cliff face. The rock was weathered, and disposed in broken slabs creating miniature caves. Though now in shadow, it had absorbed the sun's heat through the morning hours, and was now radiating the warmth it had collected.

Suddenly, he heard a shrill cry from the rear of the line. He swiveled his head. Brown and his horse were clearly in view. Brown swayed in the saddle, clutching his throat. Then Faro saw something thin whip out from the crevices in the cliff and hit at Brown's cheek. At the same time he was aware of a buzzing sound . . . it increased in volume. Faro registered a stirring and writhing in the deep shadows of the narrow valves in the cliff face . . .

There was no staying here, with God knows how many rattlers waking . . . "Ride like hell!" he called, and spurred his horse.

Books by Zeke Masters

Published by POCKET BOOKS

Most Pocket Books are available at special quantity discounts for bulk purchases for sales promotions, premiums or fund raising. Special books or book excerpts can also be created to fit specific needs.

For details write or telephone the office of the Vice President of Special Markets, Pocket Books, 1230 Avenue of the Americas, New York, New York 10020. (212) 245-6400, ext. 1760.